My Very First Story Time

Jack and the Beanstalk

Retold by Ronne Randall
Illustrated by Sophie Rohrbach

Jack

Jack's mum

man

beanstalk

castle

cow

magic beans

gold coins

giant's wife

giant

axe

ONCE UPON A TIME, in a land far away, lived Jack and his mum. They were very poor. They had no food and no money. Whatever could they do?

"All we have left is Bessie," said Jack's mum.
"You will have to take her to market and sell her."

The next day, Jack set off for market with Bessie.
On the way, he met a strange-looking man.
"That's a very fine cow," the man said.

"Will you swap her for these beans? They're magic!"
"Magic beans!" said Jack. "What do they do?"
"Just you wait and see," said the man, mysteriously.

Jack rushed home. "Mum, look!" he cried. "I've swapped Bessie for these beans. They're magic!"

"Beans?" said Mum angrily. "We need money for food, not silly old beans! Now we have no money and no cow!"

With a wave of her hand – WHOOSH! – She flung the beans out of the window. Then she sent Jack straight to bed.

When Jack woke up the next morning, he had a big surprise.
"Oh, my!" he said. "I can't believe my eyes!"

While he had slept, a giant beanstalk had grown outside his window. It reached way up high, higher than the treetops, up to the sky!

Jack rushed outside.

"I'm going to climb this beanstalk," he cried.

Up and up he went, up past the rooftops . . .

past the treetops . . . past the clouds.

At last he reached the very top,
and there he found a castle.

He knocked at the door.

With a creak and a crack the door slowly opened.
A woman stared at Jack.
"Yes?" she said.

"I'm so hungry," said Jack. "May I have some food?"
"All right," said the woman, "but my husband will be
home soon. He is a giant and he eats little boys!"

And then, the giant DID come home!

"Hide!" said the woman, pushing Jack into a cupboard.
Peeping through a crack in the door, Jack saw the giant
take out a sack of gold coins.

He started to count them . . .
"One . . . two . . . three . . ."

"So much gold!" said Jack to himself.

As the giant counted, his eyes began to close. When the giant was asleep, Jack crept out and climbed on to the table.

One . . . two . . . Jack took as many gold coins as he could carry and ran away.
But then . . .

. . . the giant woke up! The clinking and the clanking of the coins had disturbed his sleep.

"FEE FI FO FUM!" he shouted.
"I will catch you – here I come!"
Stomp! Stomp! Stomp! His big feet
thundered as he ran after Jack.

But Jack was too fast for him – the clumsy giant
could not catch up.

Jack scrambled down the beanstalk – zippity-zip!
"Mum!" he cried. "Bring the axe!"

Jack's mum chopped down the beanstalk – thwackety-
thwack! – so the giant could never climb down.

Jack and his mum were safe. The giant was gone, and they had enough gold to last all their lives and to live happily ever after!

Look at the twisting, winding beanstalk.
Which way should Jack climb it to
arrive at the fabulous feast?